Esna Malhotra

Invincible Publishers

First Printing: 2019

ISBN: 978-93-89600-04-9

Invincible Publishers

Registered Address: 201A, SAS Tower, Sector 38, Gurgaon - 122003

Don't Scream

The night is as black as the flesh of a crow
The sun is as dark as the witches' teeth
The sky is as gloomy as the ghoul's gross skin
And I am as pale as a ghost
Looking at the witches flying, turning every-body to stone.
The skeletons have risen and will not sleep
The mummies are rising from their tombs
The vampires have awakened from their coffins
And are showing their deadly fangs
The ghouls are looming over the graves
Hungry for our flesh
The bats are chittering
Don't scream, don't scream

A castle looms above us
The ghosts are all ready to attack
And the wind will howl
But I will be bold
Knights are ready to attack with their swords
The worst morning, the waorst night,

The scariest thing of my life!
Don't dare me
Don't scare me
Don't scream, don't scream

The scarecrows will walk and talk by them-
selves
The dolls resembling Annabelle
The wind will blow ferociously
And the thunder will strike
The ants, the spiders, and all the other
insects
Shall rule upon us
And the snakes will show their fangs
The witches will cackle and the blood will
fall!
Don't scream, don't scream
Spare us, don't dare us
Don't dare me
Don't scare me
Don't scream, don't scream............

Esna Malhotra

THE NIGHTMARE CLUB

(A WARM UP BEFORE WE HIT THE REAL SCARE)

CHAPTER 1

A DREAM

It was a dark and stormy night, a girl named Mellisa knocked on the door of Ms Pentiulan, her teacher.

A strong force carried her there and forced her to knock. Scared and alone Mellisa saw the door open but to her surprise, it was not Ms Pentiulan who opened it. A ghoulish face creeped out from behind the door. She stepped back scared and screamed her lungs out... Suddenly she woke up sweating in the middle of the night. She calmed herself down by saying... it was just a dream, just a dream.

Chanting those words she dozed off again, "Just a dream, just a dream... Just a dream..."

In the morning she dressed up, ate her breakfast and rushed to school, as she was late. When she reached the school, she ran to her classroom and knocked the door as softly as possible.

The door was opened by a ghoulish figure and not her teacher, Ms Pentiulan, just like her dream. She screamed.

Suddenly she realized it was a mask her teacher was wearing. "Happy Halloween!!" Said the teacher. Mellisa had almost forgotten it was Halloween. "Happy Halloween" Mellisa replied sighing.

After school she went to pick up her younger sister from the baby care. Her sister said she wanted to play more, so Mellisa slept. She dreamt that an old man was walking around her house and suddenly changed into a demon, and was trying to eat her. Terrified she ran as fast as she could. Suddenly she got up and realized her little sister was shaking her. "Let's go." said her little sister and they began their journey back home.

CHAPTER 2

THE ESCAPE

An hour after reaching home, her little sister ate all the dinner that her mother had kept for her. Her little sister was very notorious, and often blamed Mellisa for everything wrong she had done. It was a nice quiet evening and Mellisa was reading a book in her room's balcony. She was tired of reading so she decided to play badminton with her friend Andree. Andree had blond hair, was Melllisa's age and skinny. That evening she was wearing a pink top and blue shorts. She was a foodie and loved to eat and ate a lot every time she came to their house. This time when she came she didn't have a smile on her face like she always had. In fact this time she was frowning. Suddenly her face became pale and she puked on the green grass. “Eww!” Said Mellisa, “What happened to you?”

Suddenly a voice answered from nowhere, “I have devoured your friend into the land of nightmares and She will never come back.” A flash of light appeared and Andree disappeared. “Now it’s your turn, join us.”

Mellisa ran inside the house screaming, just in the nick of time or she would have disappeared, who knew where Andree went? Mellisa thought while shaking.

CHAPTER 3

CURIOUS

Next day she went to school still thinking about the voice. Curious as she was, so she asked her teacher, "Where is Andree? Has she come to school today?"

"No," replied the teacher. "Her mother called me saying she was missing."

I wish your friend good luck, hope she comes back home safely from wherever she is.

Suddenly she remembered the voice saying, "She will never come back." She was very sure now that all this was real and not a joke. For real how could something like this happen... wondered Mellisa.

Where was the land of nightmares? Who was behind all this?

Mellisa thought to herself, I have to solve all this and save my friend. I hope she's fine. Without her friend she had the darkest of days. She had no one to play with, no one to share secrets, no one to share laughs and giggles... her world had come to a standstill. She felt like a part of her was missing. She cried sometimes, Oh! Miserable days.

One day she woke up to find her room all messed up. Her drawers were opened, her clothes were scattered everywhere. She woke up confused and it looked like someone was trying to find something, but what? Mellisa had to find out for her dear friend.

CHAPTER 4

DETECTIVE MELLISA

It was Saturday, no school yippee!

The day had come for Mellisa to become a detective. She took out the map, there was no place known as the land of nightmares but there was a place known as the forest of nightmares.

She took out her flashlight, swinging her detective bag over her shoulders. The adventure had began, she rode through the streets on her bicycle and finally reached the nightmare forest.

There was a large fence around the forest. She climbed the fence and left her bicycle there, incase she disappeared. It was a very dark forest and the trees hid the sun. How much she wanted to rush back home... Oh! Such a deadly place, she thought.

She noticed that now she could not leave, as the fence grew higher behind her. Her cycle rode off by itself. She couldn't believe what she was seeing. Suddenly a light emerged from nowhere and the voice returned "Welcome to the land of nightmares, climb inside the portal of light, say goodbye to the world." The magical force in her first dream dragged her inside the light.

CHAPTER 5

THE LAND OF NIGHTMARES

When she opened her eyes she was not in the same forest, she was in a land beyond anyone's imagination. There were loads of volcanoes erupting around, demons were loitering on the streets. She found a book next to her titled "HOW TO DEFEAT THE KING OF NIGHTMARES AND FIND THE LOST ONES" The book guided her to look for a small house with drooling saliva all over it, inside the house she would find a jail where prisoners were kept.

She started her search for the house, after miles of walking the house came in view, she entered it as guided by the book and found the so called jail and two people imprisoned in it, who happened to be Andree and her sister Alora. She somehow managed to open the very heavy door and the three ran out. All of them started reading the book together now, it was mentioned that to defeat the king of nightmares you needed the sword of Azroath. Chant the spell written here and you may retrieve the sword...

ANDRO LIMBRO

CASTLAFORSME

LIOCRUNCHARE...

After saying the spell a bright flash appeared and the sword of Azroath landed in the hands of Mellisa.

CHAPTER 6

THE BATTLE

With the sword the three ran to the palace and challenged the king. As the battle began, the land of nightmares became the battlefield. Mellisa ran straight to the king and said "You do not realize your mistake," as bravely as she could. "I will destroy you!" Roared back the king.

"You look scary from the outside but from inside you are brainless," replied Mellisa. At the same time Mellisa gathered the courage and jumped on him and stabbed him with the sword.

The king moaned in pain, after a few more stabs the king was dead. The land of nightmares began to shake, any minute it could explode. Mellisa opened the book and said the spell to create the portal. When the portal opened, they walked through it. At last they were back in the nightmare forest. They ran to their respective homes. It was already Sunday morning by now.

When they reached home their mother's kissed them and told them how worried they were.

CHAPTER 7

WE WIN

On Sunday all three played together and formed a club. The club's name was, " The Nightmare Club".

Each one eloped and had to be found by the others.

"That's the time we will miss," said Mellisa.

"You're right." Both Alora and Andree agreed. Now Alora didn't play any tricks on them.

They were just like family and now they had a secret. The Secret of The Land of Nightmares...

THE HAUNTED HOUSE OF MARINA BAY

I'm Luke, Luke Paeler. I live in Marina Bay and I totally love it. It's full of excitement around all the time... pools, large parks and to top it all, some very beautiful beaches. Its wonderful here, all that you can ever imagine.

Oh! Did I mention that I'm kind of a scaredy cat. If you are too, there is one thing you won't like about Marina Bay. People call it "THE BAY SCARE" but I call it "THE HAUNTED HOUSE OF MARINA BAY". I'm not sure if every place has a scare like the house we have here...

This house is hundreds of years old. The lawn is untidy and the plants are overgrown. The roof has leaks and holes in it. Nobody lives there and hence we all suspect that it's haunted. Actually, to be honest, I have never really seen it. I am still gathering the courage to go near it but people have shared its description with me.

Last year a girl and a boy came to buy the house. It was very strange, I would say really really strange because the girl was my age and the boy was fourteen. I'm sixteen by the way. They said that they were orphans and had enough money to purchase the house. After one day of living in that house they disappeared and were never to be seen again. This was the latest news in Marina Bay.

Since no crimes like murder, disappearances, etc. ever happen here so most people say that the ghost caught them and some say they ran away because they couldn't bear the ghosts.

Both ways it was haunted for sure. The news spread across Marina Bay and the house was proved to be haunted. No one went near that house after this incident, not even the police.

Now let me tell you the story of how one day I managed to get inside it and the events that followed. Now here I was eating a really tasty lunch of Russian salad and tomato soup, it was pretty amazing.

Like a routine, after lunch I went to my friend Joe's house, he is my best friend. We plan to do something every afternoon. Sometimes we parasail, swim, run etc., it's always fun. But that day Joe had something else in his mind, something I wouldn't like. Something I will always regret.

He didn't know that I was a scaredy cat, so he asked me if I wanted to explore The Haunted House of Marina Bay. I wanted to ask him if he was crazy or something but I didn't want him to think that I was scared so I agreed to go to the haunted house of Marina Bay. That was the worst mistake of my life.

Joe and I rode our bicycles till the bay scare as Joe calls it. I was shivering not with cold but with fear. Chills ran down my back. When we reached the bay scare, I was surprised. I had imagined an old house, probably a very scary looking one with broken windows and some rickety stairs. Something that came out of a horror movie.

Instead it was a brand new house. No broken windows, no scary things. May be this is not so scary, I thought to myself. "Is that the house?" I asked Joe, pointing towards the new house. "What?" Joe said, "No it's that one." He pointed towards the third house to the left of the new house.

Well that matches my description, I muttered to myself. I admit I was very scared, I tried to calm myself but that didn't work really well. It never works, it doesn't believe me. Joe climbed up the front porch and opened the door. It made a loud creek and opened easily.

"WELCOME..." said a booming voice, it sounded like a man but I wasn't sure. I couldn't think clearly. I couldn't even breathe I was so scared. Then I realized the truth that it was Joe. He was laughing out loud... "Gotcha!" He said. Phew! I let out a sigh of relief. I thought it was the ghost. Angry and relieved I stepped into the house. Joe came after me, still laughing but when we saw the living room our emotions turned to fear. Our laughter vanished and turned to frozen pale faces.

The living room was large and bare. No furniture, totally bare except a fireplace. Cobwebs were everywhere, hung on the ceiling, on the floor; all I could see was cobwebs. The most terrifying thing of all was the fireplace. The fireplace was filled with ashes and something lay in front of it, lifeless. The thing drew Joe and me towards the fireplace. I couldn't believe what I saw. Am I dreaming? I asked myself. A dead body lay there, the dead body of a young girl. It was the young girl who came with the boy to purchase the house. I couldn't take it anymore and I fainted. A few minutes later I sat up. "What happened?" I managed to say. "You fainted," said Joe. "I was about to faint myself," he added. "There is a dead body, lets get out of here fast!" I said in a desperate voice. I started running towards the door but to our surprise the door creaked and closed. Even the latch locked by itself if that wasn't enough. Joe and I looked at each other surprised and terrified at the same

time. I couldn't believe what I was seeing. Suddenly I had an idea. "The windows!" I cried, "If we find any windows that are unlocked we can leap out of them and we'll be free. I want to get out of this." I told Joe. "Me too." He said. Joe examined the windows and I examined the girl. She matched the description of the sixteen-year-old girl who had disappeared with her brother, blond hair, green eyes, black pants and a green t-shirt. She looked like she was screaming before she died. How can this be I thought. Suddenly I heard Joe cry out in dismay "Luke! There isn't a single window that is unlocked." I couldn't believe it. Will we be locked here forever? Our whole lives? I was terrified, so terrified. Have you ever had a moment in your life when you think all is lost? Your life has ended? That's what I was thinking then. I haven't had many scary moments in my life. This is the scariest moment yet. Oh no! THIS CAN'T BE HAPPENING! I thought. I couldn't breathe. Everything was a blur. I was going to faint once again.

Control yourself Luke, I told myself control yourself. Don't let yourself faint. You can do it. You can control. I know it. I took a deep breath. Inhale, exhale, inhale, exhale. Steady. Steady. That's it Luke, that's it. Think about a way to get out of here.

Please Luke please think. How can we get out of here, how? I sat down on the floor and thought.

Suddenly I heard a girl's voice... Oh! There are more scares left, I thought to myself. I saw the dead body move and get up. It somehow managed to stand still and talk. "Oh! Finally, finally I'm awake," she cried. "Well you won't understand," she continued, "if somebody enters my house, I start haunting that person forever and ever... "

I was frozen with fear and could neither speak nor move. "My brother, he'll be waiting for me. It will be a wonderful family reunion but I'm afraid you wouldn't be able to see it."

Then she giggled and the voice echoed everywhere. "I just have to take your souls," she laughed in a raspy voice this time.

"Run! Run! I will catch you, I will."

As she said that, I had an idea. "Joe, we will run towards the backdoor in three seconds," I whispered. "There we go 3, 2, 1." We ran and we didn't look back. We just ran as fast as we could till Joe's house.

Guess what? We even forgot our bicycles.

We ran inside the house and looked through the windows. No sign of that girl. Later I walked till my house terrified and relieved but mostly terrified. I thought about telling mom and dad but I knew they weren't going to believe me, so I decided to stay quiet. I entered my room, my house keeper Ria greeted me with the usual smile. I rushed into my room, grabbed my camera and clicked a photograph of a butterfly in my book. I love photography it helps me think and calms me down. I clicked a picture of myself. I looked at myself in the picture I had brown hair, green eyes, wearing brown pants and a yellow top. I looked like a fool, I mean who wears brown pants and a yellow top it's just not a good combination. My mom called me from downstairs. "Luke, come down dinner is served."

I went downstairs to eat my dinner. It was spaghetti and meatballs. I like spaghetti but I don't like meatballs. I ate the spaghetti and took out the meatballs. I went upstairs to sleep. I hugged myself protecting myself from the cold, thinking about the incident in The Haunted House of Marina Bay. Was it even real? I thought about how the girl got up and her manly voice. I recognized that voice it sounded like... like my uncle's. Yeah! That was my uncle's voice. I remembered going to my uncle's house. It was really big. It was like a dream come true. I remember his raspy voice which I was scared of. It couldn't be. I was just imagining it and then I let myself relax and go to sleep. I dreamed about the girl and the boy chasing me through the cold frosty dark nights. I didn't know that this dream would be real so soon. Then I heard a knock on my window. I woke up, sweating. I looked outside the window and I couldn't believe what I saw. I screamed but no sound came out. The ghost of the girl from The Haunted House of Marina Bay was floating in the air right outside my window. Behind her was the ghost of the young boy who had brown hair, green eyes and wore similar clothes like his sister. The worst thing of all was that the boy was carrying Joe, who was screaming and wailing. The boy's ghost held Joe like he weighed nothing and the girl looked at me with an icy glare. That icy glare froze me in place, I couldn't move. She lifted me in her arms and carried us to The Haunted House of Marina Bay.

I couldn't speak or move or do anything.

"Now we will take revenge of what you did to us," said the girl's ghost.

"What did we do to you?" I asked, when I felt my voice coming back.

"Weren't you captured by the ghost's and they killed you?"

"Well, let me tell you a secret," said the girl

"Two young women killed us and we want to take revenge," the girl continued.

"We will take your souls, when the time is right, when the full moon shines in the night. So let me do this carefully."

"We haunted the house," continued the boy

"The women were jealous and wanted our money, they broke into the house. We heard the noise of something falling. We went to check what caused the noise and it was the two women. We saw them, they saw us and they killed us. They saw our ghosts and they ran for their lives and now you will do the same."

"You will pay! You will pay!" They chanted, circling around us.

"Why us?" I shouted over their chants.

"We want revenge on humans and you are one of them," said the girl hoarsely.

"Joe," I said, "till they are chanting let's run." "Okay." Said Joe and we started running. We ran till the front door but it was locked. We ran to the backdoor, locked as well. We checked every window in the house, locked. No way to escape, we were stuck. Stuck in an abandoned house with two ghosts who wanted our souls and revenge on mankind. I bent down on my knees for the first time in my life, I cried. I shouted for someone to help me. No one heard us, scared and alone we hid under the table. As usual, Joe tries to keep a smiling face, trying to comfort me. He always keeps a smiling face even in such situations, he asked me to calm down.

"Try not to faint." He told me. In a few minutes the boy and the girl found us. I froze once again. Then I was surprised to find a latch under the table, I opened the latch and we fell through the trapdoor, when we reached the ground, I realized we were on the street. Then we started running. I ran till I didn't know where I was and neither did Joe. It was a very deserted and dark street. I felt scared, the same feeling I had felt about a hundred times today.

"Joe," I shouted. "Lets try to find home, okay... Okay?" There was no reply.

"Joe! Joe!" I looked in the direction where Joe was standing. Nobody was there. I just stood there looking into the misty foggy night. I was left all alone. I was lost, confused, and scared. In the middle of the night standing in some weird neighbourhood with no one around to help me. I will try to locate my house I decided but which way? Should I go right, left or straight? I decided to go straight. I was too tired to run. So I walked.

I walked through the dark and dingy neighbourhood. I tried to recognize the houses around me. But nothing I saw was familiar. Suddenly I saw one familiar house. It was Tia's house. Tia was in my school. I had attended her birthday party once so I remembered this house. I should be very close to my neighbourhood. I walked and walked. It felt like hours of walking. But it was only a few minutes. I

started walking faster and faster and now I had reached my neighbourhood. I heaved a sigh of relief but then I saw something that terrified me. I saw the girl's ghost right behind me.

"Nowhere to run," she said spookily.

"Nowhere to go, you are trapped." I admitted. I was scared. I had never been so scared in my life before. If you are trapped in a neighbourhood with a ghost, how will you feel? What now? I thought. Then suddenly when the girl didn't expect it I pushed through and broke into a run. I was terrified.

"Help! Help!" I shouted as she floated above me making wild grabs for my head. All I could do was run.

"I want your soul," she kept on repeating like a chant.

"I want your soul, I want to live again." I didn't care to listen to her chants, not when I had a chance to live. As I ran I started crying. Will she kill me? I asked myself. Will I be a ghost? Will I be dead?

Will I ever see my family again? My tears fell to the ground like rain. Then I realized something. It was raining. I felt worried for Joe. I felt scared for myself. I felt glad that I had runaway. I had a feeling that maybe it was just a dream but I didn't think so because I could feel the rain. But just to make sure I pinched myself. "That hurt," I cried out. Even though I had nobody to talk to, I looked up at the sky, the girl was still above me. But she had stopped her chants. So I started running faster. My sides ached. My feet hurt. But I wasn't going to stop running unless it was eight in the morning or whenever the full moon disappears. The whole world was nothing but black and white and it was just me running in it. Everything was a blur as I ran. Still I was lost in my thoughts. I thought if I was ever going to escape or will they take my soul. I wondered if I would become a ghost. Then I started thinking about Joe. Was I ever going to see him again? I pictured Joe running like me, trying to escape from the boy's ghost. Trying to dodge, trying to hide, trying to escape but the ghost got hold of him and took him to The Haunted House of Marina Bay. The ghost cackled wildly at Joe's desperate cries. Will the same happen with me? I thought. If I escape tonight, will this same happen tomorrow night too? So many questions wandered in my mind. So many questions that I hadn't found the answers to. So many questions were in my mind. I was almost about to fall. I looked up at the sky again only to see that the girl's ghost was not there. I thought I should stop and take some rest and I did. I was very tired. Too tired. I had never run so much in my entire life. I was never a sporty kid. Once, I took part in a football match. Believe me you do not want to hear this story. I'm pretty good in studies. Do you know which grade I'm in? I'm in 10th grade. People say 10th grade is tough. But I don't think its tough. As I sat on the sidewalk, panting like a dog I thought of school. These days in school we were studying about trigonometry in mathematics, our mathematics teacher is Mrs Mia. She is kind, beautiful and everybody loves her.

Some kids have a crush on her. Then there is our English teacher Mr. Hardy. He's a jolly fellow. On the first day of school he let us do whatever we want. Cool right? Then comes our social studies teacher Mr. Maniac.

Yes his last name is Maniac. It suits him cause he is a maniac about studies. I remember his words

"Study well or..." Then he would give us a stern glare. We gulped. Joe was Mr. Maniac's favorite student. He always praised Joe. He had never praised anyone before, except Joe. He always said this child Joe is special or he said learn to be like him. That thought made me think about a night like this one. The only night in my life I was scared of. I went to find the truth. Why did Mr. Maniac like Joe? I snuck out of the house, all alone. Walked till Mr. Maniac's house. I snuck into Mr. Maniac's house by climbing inside the window. I opened the first door I saw, surprised to see who was sleeping inside. It was Joe!

"What?!" I cried! Then I had quickly run out of the house. Not sure if Joe had seen me. So I ran till my house. The next day when I went to school, I got to know that Joe had seen me. He asked me if I wanted to be friends with him. I had nodded and said, "Yeah sure."

That is how we became friends. No use of thinking about that now. He would already be dead.

Joe was Mr. Maniac's son, if you were still wondering about the connection.

When I got my head out of the clouds, I saw a sight that made me back away, a snake. I saw the black shadow of a snake slithering towards me. The green scaly skin glinting in the moonlight. Frightened I took another step back. I couldn't think of anything, so I grabbed a tree branch and managed to hit the snake with it. Then I started walking, walking as fast as I could.

What is Marina Bay at night? I thought to myself, a torture chamber. I stopped walking and started running more like jogging because I had seen the girl right above me. The boy swoops in the scene and joins his sister. "We want your soul," they chanted and then the girl spoke up. "Join us, ghosts of the night." And before I knew it, all kinds of ghosts, monsters, extraordinary creatures, all surrounded me.

A thousand ghosts chased after me. This was so scary, I was almost about to faint but I knew if I did, it would have consequences. How can I escape, I thought. There could be something I could use, there must be a way and there should be a way. Come on, I urged myself. Come up with a new idea, I started thinking as hard as I could but this time I had no solution.

I ran and ran, time passed by but the night never seemed to turn into morning, the sun never came up. The moonlight guided me in the darkness; it was the only thing I could trust. I ran faster and faster until I fell on a patch of weeds. Come on get up I urged myself, start running but my body and my feet didn't agree with my mind. Scared to death in the middle of the night, 'Death of Luke Paeler and Joe Maniac' I could imagine this title on Marina Bay's local newspaper.

Suddenly I had an idea, I got up and ran towards the closest house. Why didn't I think of this before, I thought. It was so obvious, I reached the house but I didn't check the front door I knew it would be a waste of time. I saw an open window at the back of the house and I divided into it. It was pitch dark inside, for a minute I sat down to catch my breath. I didn't care to see whose house it was. I knew I had to lock every window in the house so the ghosts couldn't come in. Will this really work I thought? No time to think I told myself. I ran up to the window I had jumped in from and I locked it. I ran out of the room I was standing in. Finally I found a light switch, now I could see which room I was standing in. It was the living room with bright pink furniture. I focused on finding the windows in the living room. I locked every one of them but what about the rooms in which the owners of this house were sleeping? I didn't want to harm their family. I had to close all the windows. All the other rooms were on the first floor, so I took the stairs to the first floor. I practically ran up the stairs, when I reached the first floor I could see a dark hallway with two doors. I entered the first door I saw, it was a large room with a king sized bed on which a little girl was sleeping. Right above the bed was a window which was wide open but luckily the girl was sleeping on the other side of the bed. Oh !Oh! I muttered when I saw the girl's ghost peep through the window. "A little girl, what a lovely feast!" Said the girl's ghost.

I was too terrified to do anything, I gathered my courage, took a deep breath and tip toed towards the bed. I climbed on the bed, I grabbed the windowsill pulled it towards me and latched the window. With a cry of surprise the girl's ghost jumped back. I was stunned by how I had defeated my fear and saved a precious life. I silently congratulated myself. I looked sideways at the girl who remained asleep, snoring peacefully. I closed the door behind me. Once again I ended up in the dark hallway. I ran towards the second door, it was the parent's room. It was cramped and small, I could see the little girl's parents. The father was snoring loudly while the mother didn't make a sound. The bed they were sleeping in was so small they could barely fit in. It seemed like the girl was sleeping in her parents room and the parents were sleeping in the girl's room. The window was right beside the bed and I let out a sigh of relief. This is going to be easy, I thought. I walked up to the window without looking at the scenery outside then I locked it. Phew! A sigh escaped my mouth. There was a small chair at the corner of the room, I sat on it to rest. All the windows of the house had been locked and the ghosts couldn't come in. I was about to sleep on the chair when something caught my eye, guess who? The ghosts of the boy and the girl. "What? How is that possible? "How did you come in?" I asked in a surprised voice.

"The chimney" the girl answered simply, it's probably a dream, I thought. I slapped myself on the face, but no it wasn't. They closed in on me, I was terrified, "No, stop right there." I heard a shout behind me, I turned around to see Joe. "Joe!" I cried happily. "Where were you?" I asked him. "I hid somewhere," Joe answered. "Where?" I asked. I was so overjoyed to see my friend that I forgot about the ghosts. "No time to talk." Joe said pointing at the ghosts. "Run!" I cried so loud that I had forgotten I was in somebody else's house. "Who's that?" A booming voice asked. I looked upward to see the father sitting straight in his bed. Joe and I both started running for our lives.

"Is our house being robbed, daddy?" I heard a voice from the next room. I was so startled and surprised that that was the last thing I heard before I fainted. Am I in heaven, I asked myself scratching my head. I felt like I had woken up from a deep sleep. I was in a large room with eight chairs and above all of the chairs was a sign that read, "Ghosts Council" I moaned in fear, whatever those words meant they were not good for me. I glanced around the room. It was a wide room with wooden furniture, it reminded me of some place but which place was it? Think Luke think, I scolded myself. Yes now I remembered, I was in the basement of The Haunted House of Marina Bay. How did this happen? I asked myself. Right when I fainted, I was being accused of being a robber, now suddenly I lay in The Haunted House of Marina Bay. I tried to get up from my chair even though no ropes were tied around me, an invisible force held me back. Beside me there was a chair on which Joe lay unconscious. I realized that we both had been kidnapped by ghosts. What a night, I tried to make sense of it all. I tried to make myself comfortable but who could be comfortable while being kidnapped by ghosts. I kept looking at Joe, hoping he would be awake any second. But my hope didn't last for long, once again I got lost in a tangle of thoughts but this time these thoughts weren't just thoughts, they were some kind of information. I didn't see ghosts council or anything in front of me, I saw the day my uncle died. I could see his black white coffin, lying in front of me, a crowd of people and two kids who were crying the most. They were children of my uncle. I remembered my aunt had died while giving birth to a girl and a boy. It was weird how I thought I had seen them somewhere, it was like my thoughts wanted me to know something but if I could only find out what that something was. Was it just a random thought? Or was it something important? Something that could make me fix my life. Was I missing something? What piece of the puzzle was I missing? My head throbbed heavily but the image of the day my uncle died still remained right in front of my eyes. Suddenly I remembered something, my uncle when he came to Marina Bay, he had bought this very house and lived in this very house. The second thing I remembered was the eighth day after my uncle died, this house in Marina Bay was claimed as The Haunted House of Marina Bay. It was all connected somehow and I

knew it now. This was scary and terrifying. Is this even happening? I asked myself. The vision of my uncle disappeared replaced by the real world. For the thousandth time in the night I screamed out "Help!" I kept screaming on and on... thinking that may be my family or friends would come to help me but I convinced myself that they wouldn't, I convinced myself that this was not a fairy tale. Suddenly out of nowhere eight ghosts appeared. "Listen up," one called "What can we do with them, we do have to take their souls but first let's do something horrible?" The other ghost's let out a cry of joy. "Burning quick sandpit it is." Said the ghost who had spoken before. The first ghost freed me and took me to a large sandpit and another one carried Joe. I was scared out of my wits. Quick sand pit sounded very scary but what was scarier was that one ghost took a match and lit the quick sandpit on fire. Another ghost led me up the ladder, the rest of them crowded around the sandpit chanting "Fiery quick sandpit!" I realized that if I jumped into that fiery pit I would burn alive. Suddenly I had an idea, I still might have a small water bottle that I had been carrying with me all this while. I could use the water to burn out the flames. I felt in my pocket and it was there. The fire was taken care of but what about the quick sandpit, I would sink under the sand and would not be able to breathe. Oh! Yes I had another idea, the ghost who had led me up to the quick sand pit had a rope in his hands, a rope to fish me out when I am fully burnt and I could use it to save my life. The ghost grunted out in surprise as I tugged the rope from his hand. He was so surprised that I got the rope and I pretended to fall into the quick sandpit. As soon as I was in the pit, I grabbed for my water bottle and then realized that it was not there. I had left it on the ladder but I still had the rope, didn't I? I realized that the rope in my hands had burnt, no way to escape again. My whole body started burning, I quickly tried to walk to the end of the quick sandpit. I tried to walk but the quick sandpit tugged me under. I took one step forward, and then the quick sandpit tugged me so hard that I went under it. I plunged into the deep darkness, knowing that I would never see earth again. Then I heard a loud cry, and I heard somebody walking towards the side of the sandpit. With the last burst of my energy, I kicked myself upwards, in time to see Joe hurrying towards me with a rope. I grabbed the rope and pulled myself up, it felt so nice to get out of the sandpit. Soon I realized that all my clothes were burnt and I had burns on many parts of my body too. I was still so grateful that Joe had come to my rescue, I owed my life to him then I remembered about all the ghosts, they were still there floating high up in the air, glaring angrily at us preparing to swirl down and grab us. Before they could do anything Joe shined a flashlight on them that made them swirl away and fly in different directions. Then Joe said "I found a way to defeat them, if you put any kind of light on them they run away afraid that it's daytime, that's how I saved you." Suddenly I started feeling cold, I felt the coldness wrap around us and then it went away. The flashlight flickered and the white light of the flashlight disappeared.

"Joe," I asked trembling "Why did the flashlight go out?" I managed to stammer, "I don't know," said Joe, "I checked the battery before coming." Suddenly the ghost's started to appear and I understood how the flashlight went off. The cold swirl that Joe and I had felt was not any other wind, it was a ghost and it had taken the batteries. We didn't know what to do so we started running. Hand in hand through the haunted house of Marina Bay. To our surprise the front door was unlocked. We ran out into the cool and fresh air of the silent night, we made our way through the bushes and the trees, through the overgrown grass and as we ran Joe fell on the overgrown roots of a tree. "Get up Joe come on," I urged him but I knew he couldn't because when Joe fell his head had hit a rock. His head oozed with blood, run Luke he cried weakly. The ghosts were coming closer, I had to choose was it Joe or was it me. I didn't think Joe could be saved so I started running. As I ran tears ran down my cheek. I know it was selfish to leave him alone but what would you do? I stopped crying and started focusing, there must be something I could do to save myself. I needed to get an idea but fast, I started screaming and shrieking but of course no one heard me. That moment I had an idea, may be I could hide. Wasn't such a good idea but it was the best I had got. I am soo scared, I searched for a place to hide. I have such a slow processing mind but at least it works. I hid behind a tree with a thick trunk, I think it was a mango tree but I couldn't think about it now. Then I remembered that it was not a game of hide and seek, I was probably hiding from thousands of ghosts, so I looked around in search of a better hiding place. My eyes searched desperately, come on come on, I urged myself. I searched and searched through gardens and fields. Unfortunately there was no other place to hide, have I mentioned I am very bad at finding things? So I decided to hide at the same hiding spot, yes I am talking about the tree. My heart pounded, my knees trembled, my body shook and I thought how could I ever escape this? In a few minutes, I heard the soft thud of footsteps. "Joe" I muttered to myself but I was wrong it was not Joe, it was the ghost of the girl. She was not flying but walking. Oh no! I am dead, I thought. "You want to play hide and seek isn't it?" The girl guffawed. Oh! I love that game and this time we are playing the second version, hide and die!" She cackled. What a wonderful name, could she read my mind? I thought. "I am coming for you, this is going to be exciting, ha! ha! ha! ha!" Her cackle echoed through the darkness of the night. Suddenly I heard a chant in the distance, somebody was chanting loudly, it was the ghost of the boy. He chanted, "I am going to suck the life out of you, we are going to make victory stew, we are going to take over your body, rule the night and you can't fight!" He chanted and chanted until thousands of ghosts surrounded me. I found myself hiding behind a tree with ghosts circling me, it made me feel dizzy, I got to admit. The ghost of the boy had made a wonderful chant, I gripped the tree tightly shivering from fear and chills ran down my back, my body was ice cold. Huff! What will I do now? Thinking this I fainted and when I came to my senses, a thousand ghosts still circled me waiting for me to open my eyes. The ghost of the girl shot a cold glare at me. With all my strength I stood up, my eyelids felt heavy. I couldn't do anything now, there was nothing I could do. The ghosts knew that too. The ghosts lurched forward towards their prey, that being me. I opened my eyes, the girl floated in the air right above me, the boy walked up to me, I gasped as soon as I saw the boy. He was human, Oh no! He had taken Joe's soul. "At last the time has come," the girl said "as I feast upon your soul and live on, you will die. As I become powerful you will become powerless." I stood there taking support of the tree, I blurted out the words, "It's only a nightmare." But I knew it wasn't. My last words on this very earth, my time had ended, my life has ended too soon, it's too soon I thought, my last thought.

A bright light shone in the sky, the last thing I saw, the bright light coming out of my chest into the sky and inside the girl's ghostly body, "The End."

Is it the end? I was sucked into the black vortex my body left behind and out of my body came my ghost. The sun had risen and my ghostly body was led into the tree, I would haunt the tree for ever and ever, I want my revenge on those brats, I won't let them go and I am not going to rest. A thin and sly smile spread over my face, I had a plan. Some people passed the tree talking about two orphans a girl and a boy I listened closely. "These orphans were found right here," one from the group said and pointed at the tree. "Which orphanage are they in?" One asked. "I don't remember," the other replied. Please remember, please remember, I prayed silently. "Ya I remember now," one of the women blurted out, "The state orphanage, its in Pasedena." Pasedena I thought, that's soo far away, so very far away. "They haven't taken them in the orphanage now," the women continued. "When are they taking them?" One asked. "Poor things, they are taking them tomorrow morning." "Where are they going to sleep tonight?" One questioned. "Very interested in these orphans aha!" The other one said. "They," the woman coughed and continued, "Are staying at Railer's Hotel on 5 Oak Lane Avenue." "Oh! Poor things poor things," the other one repeated. "May be you can call them to your house." One commented. "No, absolutely not!" Said the one in the red coat, and they walked away chuckling and giggling. I looked around, I could see five children chasing a pigeon across the lawns, I could hear laughter, I could see a girl, ice-cream cone in hand. I could see two boys riding their bikes . Oh! How I wished I could join them. Oh! How I wished I could return to my normal life again. I took a deep breath, its hard to be a tree, specially the ghost of a tree. The world seems smaller when you are a ghost. It's like a marble, the children look as small as weeds, and adults look like babies. The world is really different if you are a ghost but I admit it, it was really really very scary. You do not want to be a ghost anytime soon. I was getting really sleepy and tired, my heart felt as it was about to burst, my muscles ached. I didn't know even if I had muscles. If a ghost could faint I would have fainted by now. You know, its not fun being a ghost, not fun at all. You wish you could just walk in there and start playing with all the kids, even if you try to you can't. You wish you could fly to your house and meet your family again, but you can't. So I kept looking keeping my anger and my sadness to myself. I didn't want to terrify anyone. I just wish it could be over now, sitting on that tree alone, made me think of what I have faced. Where was Joe? Where were the ghosts? Was my family even worried about me? Did they know I was out here? May be they forgot me. May be the ghosts made them forget me. I didn't see any missing signs, but after thinking over my revenge plan, my revenge plan on those two ghosts. Thinking and thinking the lights faded, the world darkened and you couldn't even hear a pen drop in the silence of the night. I have never liked silence and silence has never liked me. I took a deep breath and I knew what I had to do, it was really important to me. You can imagine I didn't want to live all alone, all alone in this darkness. I didn't want to live by hiding, by knowing I wouldn't have a future. I wanted revenge, vengeance of what those two did to me, even though I was experiencing their pain, I didn't have any mercy on them. My eyes filled with tears, they grew an angry red as the world pulled me to darkness. An angry cry burst from my throat, "I want revenge," I cackled. "Revenge, revenge, revenge," was all I chanted, "Revenge, revenge." I rasped. I didn't know it but I was becoming evil, I was becoming a ghost. I wanted my life back and I was going to fight for it, I floated up into the air leaving the tree behind knowing I would never see the tree again, but I could be wrong. As I floated what fun I had, the cold night breeze was blowing. My hair brushed against the wind and I couldn't help myself, I let out a cry. A cry of agony, a cry of somebody who has been betrayed but then I stopped. Really Luke, I asked myself, you are turning into one of them but I couldn't stop myself. I rushed through the air like wind. After four minutes of flying I reached, I finally reached. I stared down at Railer's Hotel, Oak Lane Fifth Avenue. The time had come to face my fear, to take back what was mine, just one advice "Sharing is not caring." I went up to the desk in the main hall of the hotel, the desk attendant was sleeping soundly. I glanced over the register, a brown leather book. I don't know how I was going to find the room, but I was .I glanced at first floor, then second floor turning the old yellowed pages. Hoping as I turned over the pages, then I turned over to the third page that was dated today but then I spotted it, the last room number listed on the page, it was 363. Beside it was written State Orphanage, Pasedena orphans. Yes! Then I floated on the stair passage towards the third floor, floated through the yellow and pink wallpaper halls. "Ha, ha, ha," I cackled, "Oh boy! This is going to be fun. The greatest moment in history, so I approached the door, the black leathered door and pulled it open. As I peeked into the room, I thought the boy and the girl were certainly not expecting me or were they. Let's find out, we soon will. I came right in, I gazed over the room, unpacked suitcases, clothes thrown every where like they were in a hurry, weird .The only thing that mattered to me was that they were both sleeping in there comfy, cozy beds under their blue pink blankets. It reminded me of home, home sweet home, now gone because of the people or may I say ghosts sleeping in their beds right in front of me. They didn't deserve this, I did, this was not right. "Souls," I rasped hungrily. I twisted my hand weirdly like I was a magician doing magic. I didn't even know what I was doing, it was like I was not controlling me but someone else was. I felt uncomfortable, I know why now, I really had to go to the bathroom, but I controlled it. Not now I told myself.

Anyway as I moved MY hand in that strange weird way, a white light came out of the girl just like it had came out of me the other night, I still remembered that moment, it's painful but it didn't go inside me like it did inside the ghost of the girl. Am I doing something wrong I asked myself, what if I am never able to do this, what if I will always be a ghost sitting on that tree in the day all alone and roaming through the streets floating crying all alone. No, no I told myself, this will happen, I know it will. Tears sprang in my eyes, I can't do this I realized but my faith, and my thirst for revenge reminded me how much I wanted this. I will not fail, I will not take no for an answer. YOU can do this Luke or can you, I took a deep breath gathered my courage and once again started moving my hand. If somebody saw me do this, I would look like a wierdo I thought. So, I locked the door and went back to my procedure. Now nothing could stop me but something could, something I hadn't noticed because I was so caught up in my emotions. The

white light wasn't coming out of the girl, it was coming from a flashlight from inside the blanket. How could I not notice this? I scolded myself. How could I not notice that the girl and the boy had tricked me, I pulled the sheet off from whom I thought was the girl, a dummy, it was a dummy under the sheet. The dummy started at me lifelessly. I felt dizzy, I fell to the floor and collapsed. Suddenly I woke up sweating in the middle of the night, it was all a dream. I glanced at my alarm clock it is 03:00 in the morning it seems so real. How could I be so foolish to believe my dream? But what, I did not know what was about to happen in reality. My room suddenly felt cold like a cold wind had swept through my window. I covered myself with my blanket. The cold wind was coming from above me. So I looked at the ceiling and I couldn't believe what I saw. The girl's ghost was hovering above me. I screamed. "Surprise," she cackled her ugly cackle. I gulped. "Now let's get to business. Oh I feel sorry for you. So I am going to tell you a secret...

our names because we are your cousins, your long lost cousins, Maria and Ned Paler." Yes I had heard those names. My long lost cousins. That's what my mind, my memory wanted to tell me in my dream. It was all connected. "Wha?" I was in the middle of my sentence when the ghost of the girl sucked my soul out of me.

THE END